From
Grandma & Monk Shrock
Sept. 1971

NOBODY'S BIRTHDAY

NOBODY'S BIRTHDAY

Written by

ANNE COLVER

Illustrated by

MARVIN BILECK

Alfred A. Knopf · *New York*

L. C. Catalog card number 59–10020

THIS IS A BORZOI BOOK, PUBLISHED BY ALFRED A. KNOPF, INC.

For
Stephen Colver Harris
With Love

NOBODY'S BIRTHDAY

ONCE there was a Birthday on our street.

It had balloons and party hats and paper
snappers, and a lot of presents. It had a

great big present and a tiny little present
(so small it simply couldn't be anything)

and a fat round present and a long thin
present. All of them were wrapped in tissue
paper and tied with bright colored ribbons.

It had ice cream: pink, white and chocolate, and a birthday cake with candles.

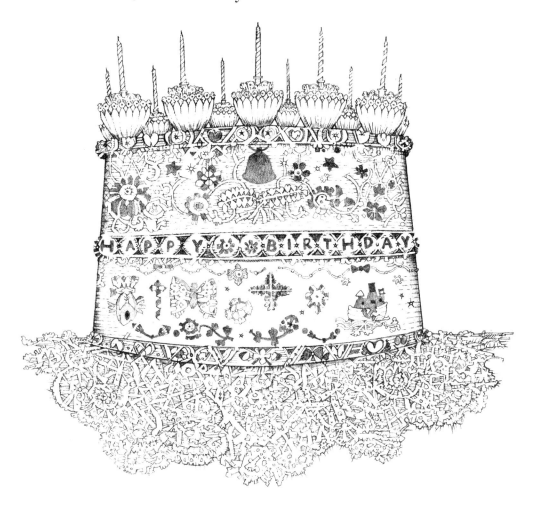

But there was something very strange
about this Birthday. It didn't belong to
anyone.

There wasn't anyone to play with the
balloons or to put on the party hats.

There
was no one to snap the paper snappers or
to open the big present or the tiny present
or the fat present or the thin present.

Nobody was going to eat the ice cream :
pink, white and chocolate.

Nor blow out the candles on the cake.
Because it was *nobody's Birthday*.
It was very mysterious.

All the children began to worry about it. They got together in a back yard to talk it over.

They said, "It must be some-
body's Birthday, but whose can it be?"

They knew it wasn't one of theirs.
They had already had their birthdays.

Danny said it couldn't be his mother's birthday because hers was two weeks ago. And Joan said it didn't belong to her daddy—his was last week.

So they thought and thought about who the Birthday might belong to and, finally, they remembered the brand new baby in the pink house half-way down the block. He was such a little baby, they thought maybe he hadn't had time to have a birthday yet. They asked the baby's mother, being very careful to whisper because the baby had just had his bottle and was sound asleep in his carriage on the porch.

The baby's mother whispered back.
"No," she told the children, "it's very kind

of you to think of him, but it isn't the baby's birthday. Even the smallest baby has a birthday all ready and waiting on the day he's born. I'm sure I can't imagine who the Birthday could belong to."

The children tiptoed away, feeling very disappointed and puzzled about the Birthday that did not belong to *anyone*.

"Somewhere," they said, "there must be somebody who doesn't have· a birthday. We must find who it is."

They started down the street to look.

First they came to the Smiling Policeman who stood on the corner.

They asked him, "Smiling Policeman, you know all the children who go to school. Do you know one who doesn't have a birthday?"

The Smiling Policeman went on smiling while he thought. "Why no," he said. "Big and little, fat and thin, I help all the children across my street. But of all those children, I never helped one who didn't have a birthday."

Next the children asked the Smoking Fireman who was busy polishing his red fire engine beside the red brick firehouse. They said, "Smoking Fireman, you drive your red fire engine all over town and rescue people. Have you ever rescued anybody who has no birthday?"

The Smoking Fireman smoked his pipe.
Finally he said, "I do drive all over town,
but I have never yet rescued anyone who has
no birthday."

Then the children saw the Whistling Mailman coming around the end of the street, and they ran to meet him. "Whistling Mailman, Whistling Mailman," they all called together. "You are *just* the one we want to see. You carry packages and post cards and letters for everybody. Do you know *one* person who hasn't any birthday?"

The Whistling Mailman looked at the children and stopped whistling. First he scratched his head, then he rubbed his chin, and then he squinted up his eyes.

Slowly, he said, "No—not one person. All the people that I carry packages and post cards and letters to have birthdays. But I'll tell you something—"

The Whistling Mailman crooked his finger and all the children came closer to listen.

"I'll tell you this," he said. "Down at the end of the street and around the corner

is a house with a row of sunflowers in the garden. On the porch, sitting in a rocking chair and whittling sticks, is the Old Man. He is *so* old that he can remember everything. Maybe he can help you."

The children said happily, "Thank you,

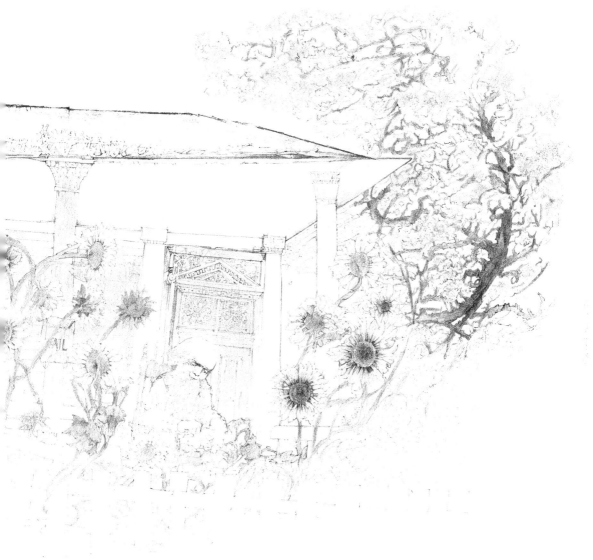

Whistling Mailman. We'll go and find him right away.''

There was the house. On the front porch, sitting in a rocking chair and whittling sticks, was the Old Man.

They stood watching until the Old Man looked up. "Hello children," he said, "what can I do for you?"

"Is it true," they asked him, "that you are so old that you remember everything?"

"I am old," he said. "Yes, I am very old." He stopped for a long time while he thought about how old he was. "I am so old that I can remember when the pussy willows were only kitten willows. I can remember Santa Claus before he had a beard and the shooting stars when they first started target practice. I remember the fish when they were learning how to swim and the birds when they still took singing lessons. I remember when the snow first became cold and the grass started being green and water was first wet. I remember all those things."

"Well," said the children, taking a long breath, "if you remember all those things, then surely you must remember someone who doesn't have a birthday. Don't you?"

The Old Man sighed. Then he shook his head.

"I can remember the biggest tree that ever grew in a forest," he said. "It was so big you could drive a horse and carriage through a hole in its trunk, and it was so tall that no one ever saw all the way to its top—but it had a birthday. And I remember the littlest minnow that ever was born in the littlest pond, but it had a birthday, too.

I remember bees

and elephants

and puppies

and all the children in the world, but of all those, there wasn't one that didn't have a birthday."

"Please," the children said, "try harder. Try to remember just one."

The Old Man tried. He tried so hard that his eyebrows quivered and the rocking chair stopped rocking, and he put down his whittling. Finally, he gave up.

"No," said the Old Man, "I have thought of every single thing and everything has a birthday. Why, even *I* had a

birthday once. Only it was so very long ago,
I must have lost it somewhere.''

Suddenly, the children caught their
breath in surprise. "Oh," they said. They
looked at the Old Man very hard, and then
they looked at each other. They began to
clap their hands because at last they knew
where the Birthday on the street belonged.

"Close your eyes tight," the children said to the Old Man. "We have a big surprise for you."

When he opened his eyes, there was the Birthday that belonged to him. The Old Man was surprised and pleased and the children were pleased too. Now it was somebody's Birthday; they could play with the balloons and put on the party hats and snap the paper snappers.

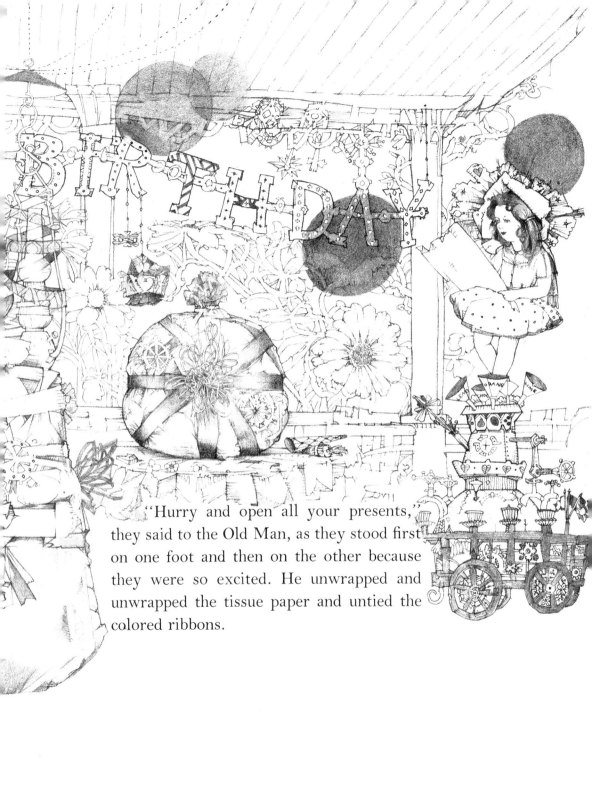

"Hurry and open all your presents," they said to the Old Man, as they stood first on one foot and then on the other because they were so excited. He unwrapped and unwrapped the tissue paper and untied the colored ribbons.

First the Old Man opened the great
big present and it was a nice new rocking
chair. Next he untied the tiny little present

(so small it couldn't possibly be anything)
and there was a new sunflower seed to plant
in the garden row. Then he undid the fat
round present and found a fat round bunch of

sticks to whittle. And finally, he unwrapped
the long thin package and it was a new bright,
shiny knife for whittling.

The Old Man was very happy. "My presents are just what I wanted," he said, "every single one. Of all the birthdays that I can remember, this is the very nicest one."

So the children put on the party hats and snapped the snappers and helped the Old Man eat the ice cream: white, pink and chocolate. They all sang *Happy Birthday* and the Old Man took a huge, big breath and blew out all the candles on his birthday cake.

"Wish for many more birthdays," the children said.

And the Old Man did.